Fritz and the Beautiful Horses

Fritz and the Beautiful Horses

Written and Illustrated by

Jan Brett

A TRUMPET CLUB SPECIAL EDITION

for my mother and father

Published by The Trumpet Club
666 Fifth Avenue, New York, New York 10103

Copyright © 1981 by Jan Brett

ISBN 0-440-84399-5

This edition published by arrangement with
Houghton Mifflin Company
Printed in the United States of America
October 1992

1 3 5 7 9 10 8 6 4 2
UPR

Once there was a walled city known for its beautiful horses.

There were magnificent jumpers, splendid chargers, and elegant
parade horses.

The citizens were so proud of these horses that it was decreed that only the most beautiful would be allowed in the city. All others would have to stay outside.

One of these was a pony named Fritz.

Fritz was not beautiful. He had a long, tangled mane, whiskers on
his muzzle, and short legs. But Fritz was very gentle and kind.
He was sure-footed and always willing to work.

Day after day, Fritz watched the beautiful horses. Some had braided manes and tails, and carried lovely ladies. Others had glossy coats and pulled grand carriages.

Most of all he watched the children's horses.

"I wonder why the children look so frightened?" he thought.

The children were afraid. They didn't like their horses prancing and leaping. It made them very difficult to ride.

As Fritz watched he thought, "I would like a child to ride me."
But no one ever noticed Fritz.

One day he climbed up to the road leading to the walled city.
He tried to take long, graceful strides. He pranced and curved his
neck. He threw his tail into the air.

The citizens stared at Fritz and then they began to laugh.
"Look at that silly horse," they said.

Then the lovely ladies and the magnificent gentlemen galloped away
toward the walled city. The children followed reluctantly behind.
"I guess I do look silly," thought Fritz and he hung his head in despair.

Fritz listened to the citizens as they galloped their horses faster and
faster. He heard their loud cheers as they rode onto the bridge
to the walled city.

All of a sudden he heard a loud SNAP. The bridge was breaking under the weight of the horses' pounding hooves.

Fritz saw a large crack appear in the middle of the bridge.

The citizens were on one side and the children were on the other.

"You'll have to cross through the river," cried the citizens.

But the children wouldn't move.

"My horse might shy and buck," said one.

"My horse might leap and stumble," said another.

"We might fall off," they all cried together.

"Stay where you are," shouted the citizens. "We will come and get you."

But their horses wouldn't move.

"This hill is much too steep," thought one horse.

"My lovely mane might get tangled in the bushes," thought another.

"We certainly don't want to get wet," all the horses agreed.

Everyone wondered what to do. Then they noticed Fritz.

Fritz carefully climbed to where the children waited.

Fritz was not beautiful, but he was gentle and kind. He was sure-footed and always willing to work. The children were not afraid to ride him.

One by one Fritz carried the children carefully down the steep hill.
He calmly stepped through the river from rock to rock and
up the other side.

He finally carried all the children to the walled city.

A great cheer went up from the citizens.
The lovely ladies cried, "Hurray for the sure-footed pony!"
The gentlemen said, "How kind and dependable he is!"

And the children exclaimed, "We didn't fall off!"
So Fritz was given a special place in the walled city.
All the children cared for him and became his friends.

From that day on, the walled city was known for its beautiful horses
and its very dependable pony.